What's Your Sound OUND the HOUND?

by
MO WILLEMS

Balzer + Bray
An Imprint of HarperCollinsPublishers

What's your sound Hound the Hound?

Woof!

Woof!

What's your sound, Chick the Chick?

Peep!

What's your sound. Cow the Cow?

What's your sound Bunny the Bunny?

Sounds like . . .

somebody
needs a hug!

To Trixie, who can make

all kinds of sounds

Balzer + Bray is an imprint of HarperCollins Publishers.

Library of Congress Cataloging-in-Publication Data
Willems, Mo.
    What's your sound, Hound the Hound? : a Cat the Cat book / by Mo Willems. — 1st ed.
        p.   cm.
    Summary: Cat the Cat's animal friends make many different sounds.
    ISBN 978-0-06-172844-0 (trade bdg.) — ISBN 978-0-06-172845-7 (lib. bdg.)
    [1. Animal sounds—Fiction.] I. Title.   II. Title: What is your sound, Hound the Hound?
PZ7.W65535Wh 2010   2009014410
[E]—dc22   CIP
                                                                                AC

Typography by Martha Rago
10 11 12 13 14 LPR 10 9 8 7 6 5 4 3 2 1
❖
First Edition